The
Maiden
of Avril

The Maiden of Avril

A COLLECTION OF STORIES AND POEMS

J. B. SCOTT

authorHOUSE®

AuthorHouse™
1663 Liberty Drive
Bloomington, IN 47403
www.authorhouse.com
Phone: 1 (800) 839-8640

Published by AuthorHouse   07/28/2015

ISBN: 978-1-5049-2251-7 (sc)
ISBN: 978-1-5049-2250-0 (e)

ACKNOWLEDGEMENTS

To my childhood friend and world's most annoying little brother. Here's to the imagination of children and time well spent.

1. NOW

"Your father is dying?"

"Dying?"

"I mean if you do not help him he will die."

"No." She trembled.

"Yes." He whispered.

"Help him how?"

"He can only get well with the tea made from this flower.' Teniah held it out to her. It was white with small black dots and pink leaves. "He said you can find more of these. That you know where to look."

"Yes. I know." Holly took the flower delicately in her palm. "It is called La fleur de nuit, night flower. It only buds at night, which is the only time it can be picked."

"How far away is it?"

"Not far, a day's journey toward the setting sun." She turned to him, saw his eyes darting back and forth eyeing her friends. She had forgotten how imitating they looked.

"We should go now," He shifted his weight to the other hoof.

"I will show you on the map." She walked around her makeshift throne to the back wall. "But I cannot come with you." She pushed in a glazed blue brick; a section of the wall shifted and slid out of the way to reveal rows and rows of stacked scrolls. Taking one of them she said, "Here in the middle of the Leto Mountains there is a waterway that runs through it, that is where La fleur de nuit grows."

"I don't understand; why aren't you coming with me? Maybe you don't understand. He's ill, very ill."

"This is where I belong. This is my home. I cannot leave"

"No Avril is your home. I've traveled night and day trying to find you. You can't stay here your kingdom needs you."

She stiffened, biting down on her lip, "I think it's time for you to go. Eureka, make sure our guest finds his way out." Then speaking to Teniah, "We wouldn't want you to get lost." A caracal moved toward him from her post. Her pupils narrowed as she closed in. He took slow, cautious steps backwards. He could see that her head and tail were up, her ears up and out like she was hunting. Once she had backed him out of the castle Eureka sat guarding the entrance, her green eyes dazzling in the moonlight as she watched Teniah disappear into the forest.

Inside Holly looked at the map; she traced her finger across it. Pass the Leto Mountains she came to Avril. He was wrong; it was a place that had never *really* been her home.

Ill. Dying. Help him. Father.

She was confident her visitor could find the flower alone. They didn't need her help.

No one did.

The rain fell heavy in the morning but he didn't care. If he couldn't go inside then neither was he leaving here without her. So he waited. He stood resolute like a solider guarding treasure. Finally the heavy oak door opened, Holly emerged, shielded from the rain by an awning at the front of the castle. She stopped cold when she saw him. He hadn't left like she thought he would. A moment passed between them; then several. One thing became clear to Holly: he wasn't leaving and she wasn't going.

Teniah laid his head back against the rough bark of a tree. Another one of her friends appeared at her side, this time a lynx named Skandia, rubbed herself against Holly's leg in ownership of her. Her loving attention stopped as she sensed a threat to her environment. Skandia turned her nose up to sniff the air; she caught his damp scent carried on the wind. She sat at her mistress's side not trusting her alone with him. Although she seemed to relax knowing it was only him. She glanced across the field with no more idle curiosity.

Holly turned to go back inside but stopped at the door to look back at him. Then with a nod of her head she gestured him to follow. Skandia trotted at her side. She stopped when she stopped, walked when she walked.

Teniah shook off the wetness. "Thanks, it was staring to get cold out there."

"The rain will let up soon and then you can be on your way."

"A man's life is hinged on your willingness to help, a man who gave you life. I can't do this alone. I may get lost or look in the wrong place. Please."

"I don't want him to die but I don't really see how I can help. I've never been there. I read about it a long time ago in a book." She handed him back the flower he had left behind.

"Come anyway, I've already lost so much time trying to find you that I don't know how much longer he can live." His voice trailed off, he was practically begging. She thought of her sick father.

"The flower where it grows is said to be dangerous. "Legends of flowers" said that it is guarded by fearsome monsters but this has never been confirmed. My friends will accompany us for protection."

"Thank you."

She ducked off into another room. She didn't know which she would regret more. Going or *not* going. She grabbed worn satchels for them both. She reappeared handing him one and put the map inside of hers.

"Dear friends, I will be gone for an extended period." She addresses the cats. He saw the caracal from last night, she was passive but a cat like that could catch a bird in midair. With a skill set like that he didn't want to think what she could do to him.

"Skandia, Tibet, Armin, Oz and Jetta you come with us." A sand cat – Tibet stepped forward. His fur was sand color with the exception of the blackish bars on his front limbs and two black rings on his tail. Then a liger followed by a lion; *Armin* and *Oz* he presumed. "Jetta will be your guardian on this quest." An Asiatic golden cat circled him rubbing herself against him and purring. He looked down at his hind legs with a mixture of fear and disgust.

The rain stopped but the cold didn't. Holly led the pack toward the west, where the sun would set that evening.

She looked back at him, they hadn't officially met. He had showed up unannounced and uninvited. She had kicked him out in the most inhospitable manner, then felt bad and let him back in. In turn, he had convinced her to come with him.

"You said you name was Ty?"

"Teniah, my lady."

"I'm not *my lady*, just Holly. So you work for my father. An advisor maybe or a noble at court."

"No my vocation is entertainment."

"Oh you mean acrobatics?"

"No, contact juggling and coin manipulation." He pulled a coin from a small purse strapped to his waist by a belt. He rolled the coin across his knuckles then switched and did it on his second hand, then back to the first. Seemingly out of nowhere he had a second coin. He rolled them on both hands effortlessly.

Teniah put the coins away and took out a glass orb which he positioned on the back of his hand and rolled it up his arm, across his chest, down his other arm and back on to his first hand. Around and around his body it went. He even made it go around his shoulders. Holly watched him do this a couple of times before he stopped it in the crock of his elbow and tossed it to the other then back to his first elbow. He held it there like it was a pet.

"Bravo." She clapped. "Very good."

He shrugged, as if none of it mattered. Just something he picked up nothing he'd work that hard at.

"I usually have a bigger act with more of these." He spun the ball around in his hand. How long had it been since she'd seen her own kind, months perhaps, years. Norks came in all shapes and sizes; all colors and furs. But he had to be the most peculiar Nork she'd seen yet. His ears stuck out of his head, he had two goatees on either side of his chin, hair that hung off his outer arms and even more hair on his legs (almost woolen) which bent funny. He had hair almost everywhere except chest and back. His feet looked funny too, cloven with no toes. As they walked he swatted flies away from his legs with his tail. Until she saw the movement she had forgotten about the tail. His feral habiliments made him look animalizing, yet homespun at the same time.

She preferred the company of four-legs now rather than those with only two. The two-legs, Norks were cruel and unfeeling; unfeeling and cruel. Wasn't any wonder she didn't want to go back. Or why she had left in the first place.

She wondered how it all began, her earliest memories. It was all her father's doing, of course. But to tell the past she would have to except some responsibility. Some of it was her fault, maybe most of it; perhaps all of it. Though she had tried and tried to un-write the past; her history was written in blood.

2. THEN

She closed one real tight and made a wish, the same wish she always made, the only wish she ever made. She relaxed the muscles in her face and looked in the mirror; there was no marked improvement in her features but maybe when she woke up. Maybe when she woke up she'd look different, she look like her mother and then her father would love her. He wouldn't push her away and yell at her. He would forgive her. She didn't know any better. She never meant to hurt anyone.

She crawled under the covers, so warm and fluffy. She tucked herself in and let her head fall back on the pillow. The waves of her fiery orange hair flowing surrounded her.

The sun beckoned from behind the window panes the next morning, waking Princess Holly to start a new day. She hoped her looking-glass would reflect a different image but she was disappointed. She was eight, everything around her was changing and she felt left behind.

The tutoress lectured on and on about the benefit to knowing poetry. She wasn't listening.

Why couldn't they have studies outside? Princess Holly thought.

She didn't care for poetry. She didn't want to recite them out loud for others to hear. All those words were so long and all sounded alike and none of them made sense. She imaged herself trying to recite a few verse and her tongue tying itself into an enormous knot. But if they could just be outside in the courtyard then she would recite till her tongue tied up on her and her eyes crossed and her face turned blue and her knees knocked and … and…

"Princess Holly. How will you ever be queen if you don't pay attention?"

It seemed that there were always things to learn. She had a tutor for every subject to teach her art, music, math, science, geography, etc. Countless servants just for her; waiting on her hand and foot. Two nannies to fetch and carry at her biding. Princess Holly was regularly presented with new gifts from members at court and other royalty in distant lands. Clothes and toys as many as her heart desired.

When her studies were done the servants had all sorts of activities and games for her to learn and play. She soon became an expert in charades. They all agreed she was better than any actor at Play.

But it was all a distraction. It was all to keep her from the one person she wanted most in the world. But, there were ways around that. She hid her favorite doll under the cushions in the sitting parlor.

"Nanny Fig I've lost my favorite dolly."

"Where did you last have it then child?"

"I don't remember. Will you find it for me?

"Yes but stay here with Nanny Noor."

"No." She said firmly. "You have to both search for it and all the servants because it could be anywhere."

Nanny Fig shock her head. "We'll all look for it; expect Nanny Noor who must stay here. You can't be left on your own." Princess Holly screamed and stomped her feet. "No! Find it now."

"Yes Princess Holly." The curtseyed and scampered away.

With no one to stop her she left the nursery. She wandered up and down the halls until she came to the right room. The door was ajar and she could hear voices coming from inside.

"This decree is to be sent to all provinces in Avril."

"Yes Your Majesty."

Princess Holly peeked into the room. She saw a woman holding a quill pin sitting at a desk. On the other side of the room a couple of men shuffling papers around. Then she saw *him*. His back was to her but she knew it was him. Although she didn't get to see him often, she could pick him from a crowd

The woman saw her. She smiled at the woman but she didn't smile back instead her eyes widened and she looked away. She thought she was pretty. She had a seal pelt that wrapped around her shoulders and down her waist and hips like a mini dress. Then he turned around to face the woman and Princess Holly could clearly see him. He was said to be the most handsome man in the kingdom. She hadn't seen everyone in the kingdom but he was the most handsome man she had ever seen and she was proud to call him her father. He had ash-blond hair, blue eyes and darkly tanned skin.

As he started to speak to the woman he noticed her uneasiness. He turned this way and that to look for the cause. That's when he saw her watching them. Before he could say anything Princess Holly felt a presence behind her and looked up to see nanny Noor standing over her. Nanny Noor could see the displeasure in the kings' face and quickly pulled the princess away.

In the nursery Nanny Fig waited along with several exhauster servants. When nanny Noor brought Princess Holly in she could see no one was the least bit happy. Least of all nanny Fig and it was not hard to guess why. In her spindly hands she held the doll.

She often played tricks on her nannies to get away and see her father. But things usually didn't go the way she wanted them to. When she turned 12 that all changed, for the good and bad.

She found her father wandering in the conservatory. He paced slowly, deep in thought. Occasionally he stopped to examine the petals of a flower, pick off the dead leaves (the gardeners had missed), or simply smell one that had freshly bloomed.

She descended the balcony steps walking toward him. By the time the guards saw her it was too late. He jumped back, shocked to see her there; shock to see her standing so close. The guards rushed up, ready to drag her away, out of his sight. Kicking and screaming if need be.

He put his hand up and they halted their pursuit.

"Hello father. I mean Your Majesty." She curtseyed. "Thank you for the pearls. It is the most beautiful gift I've ever received." She fiddled with it as it hung from her neck.

He blinked quickly a couple of times, nervously licked his lips.

She continued. "I love this place. Was it your idea to build this?"

"Oh yes." He looked over her and raised a brow. She had thought the king was signaling the guards to give them privacy. Only one left the room though. But it didn't matter, this meeting was long overdue. "I've always been found of varies species of plant life. I've collected different types from all over Avril and beyond."

"And which is your favorite?"

He had been looking up, watching the balcony. He seemed to be waiting for something but when he heard her question he immediately looked down.

"La fleur de nuit, a flower worthy of its name. I had it brought to me as a present for my bride …" His voice trailed off. Then something changed in him.

All she could do was peer up at him, hoping he continue talking. She had never felt so close to him.

"You shouldn't be here." His voice was stern. "This is *our* place. Not yours." As he said that his lips began to quiver.

"Princess!" She heard a voice behind her and the sound of hastening steps. "How many times have I told you never to leave the east wing?" It was nanny Fig, her long knobby arms reached out for Princess Holly.

"And how many times have I told you never to let her out of your sight?" The king cut in. He seemed more in control of himself. Do you know how much damage can be done be letting this child loose?"

"Yes Your Majesty."

"It has become clear to me that no one can follow a simple rule. I am busy. I do not have time for this nonsense. Don't let it happen again."

"Yes Your Majesty. I'm sorry. It won't happen again."

"Keep her contained." His eyes were as cold as iceberg.

The Princess' heart sank in her chest. *Contained.* Never again would she try to get her father's attention.

But she couldn't help knowing. The library in the east wing, her wing was rarely used. She didn't care much for reading. Her studies gave her all the reading she needed.

She climbed the ladder and scanned shelf after shelf of books. Then finally saw it. It was a brown, hard-covered book with floral designs. In gilded gold it read "Legends of flowers."

She climbed down, picked a comfortable chair, opened the book to the L section and read.

3. NOW

"Were here." she said staring straight ahead at the foggy enclosure.

The sun had disappeared behind the mountains and the dusk of the evening made the place look eerie. Little rough bumps began to form Teniah's arm.

"Oz. Armin. You two stay here."

He hated them, especially the big ones but now he wished they were coming with them. Whatever was out there was probably much worse than Holly's gracile felines.

Holly pealed back the moss tip branches and stepped inside. Skandia and Tibet followed her lead but Jetta remained motionless at his side, staring into the unknown. He felt like throwing up but that would have to wait. He stepped inside the forest enclosure; every branch seemed to jump out at him snagging his fur. He tried taking his mind off of this by focusing on Jetta's beautiful pale cinnamon coat, it helped but not much.

Holly stopped; in front of her was a waterway too deep to cross.

"Now what?" asked Teniah.

"You stay here while I go find a shallow place to cross." She could see the waterway would narrow if she followed it north.

The fog cleared in the middle where they were and encircled them like a coiling snake. The exit obstructed from view. It was getting darker. "We should stay together it would be safer."

"Don't worry, Jetta will protect you. Won't you?" Holly walked to the Asiatic golden cat and bent down to her level. "Of course, cause you a good girl." She cupped her face with her hands, nestling Jetta's face into her own. She stood back up and said "pick as many as you can. I'm going over there, not far and pick some on the other side. We don't have a whole lot of time so let's get started."

"Wa… pick what?" All he could see was damp mossy ground.

"You'll see." She smiled. "Wait for it." She disappeared in the fog with Tibet and Skandia.

The darkness was becoming over powering with every second. "Wait for what, I don't see anything." Before he finished something between the moss began to move. All around him the ground seem to be shifting and rising. Pink leaves emerged from the ground revealing a black bud, the bud pealed itself back and he could see white petals with small black spots. He was hypnotized by what he saw. It was beautiful. The flower's center belched out a tiny pearl of purple light. Everywhere purple lights floated up toward the darkened sky.

"The flower of night." He whispered, forgetting his trouble and fear. Jetta too seemed distracted by the light.

Holly crossed to the other side. As the flowers opened she worked quickly to snap off the heads as soon as the light left it. Tibet chased the light, trying to catch it in his paws before it went up. Skandia though played look out.

The mist swirled around what appeared to be the mouth of a cave. Holly saw it, saw Skandia sitting on her haunches staring into it. Then she moved on sensing it was safe. She formed a small half-moon perimeter around Holly. Pacing back and forth, she stopped occasionally to look at the waterway on the opposite back.

Holly was still crouched down; she had finished picking the ones around her. The satchel was almost full, she could pick more but what she had gathered plus whatever Teniah picked would be sufficient.

The cave stretched into utter darkness beyond the range of light. *It* rose out of the dimness to cast a grotesque black shadow as it closed in on her.

Skandia stopped her pacing. She sensed the danger but it was impossible to know exactly where it was coming from. So many shadowed hiding places, the ground fog made everything seem sinister.

Outside the enclosure Armin and Oz rose to their feet. Something was wrong, it wasn't safe.

Holly wasn't safe.

They broke orders and ran in.

They ran pass Teniah and Jetta; they were fine. Teniah turned to see them, "Where are they going?" But Jetta wasn't paying attention. She was suddenly very serious. She was looking across the water, the fog made it impossible to see the other side. Then the water rippled and everything around them was deathly calm. Jetta's tail started slashing from side to side, a low growl rumbling from her chest. Her vocalization heightened, she began hissing and spitting.

Tibet stopped playing as he and Skandia witnessed a most horrific sight. A huge beast pounced on top of Holly; she tried to run away. She tried to push it off but she was no match. It went for her ankle, biting down hard; it forcefully dragged her backward into its cave. Skandia and Tibet rushed to her aide; biting at the creatures fur. It kicked them both aside with strong legs.

Holly screamed. Teniah heard that scream and ran in that direction. Jetta followed at his heels.

Oz and Armin spilt off, jumping across the water. Armin went for the head; Oz the hindquarters. It shirked in pain, releasing Holly. She made a run for it; right into Teniah.

Before he could ask her if she was alright he saw behind her a large beast not corresponding to any actual animal he'd ever seen before.

He nearly fainted.

He did faint.

He remembered nothing after that, just waking up on the cold damp grass, still foggy from the previous night. As he was coming to his senses, he smelled something flowerlike but no flower he'd ever smelled before. As his eyes adjusted to being awake he realized what he smelled was her. She was lying next to him, her hair underneath his head. She smelled good. She looked peaceful, no trace of last night's scare on her face. Her ankle was wrapped with the same fabric as her cloak. He could see where she ripped it from the hem. He didn't remember her doing that. The wound had bleed through the powder blue cloth.

He leaned into the nape of her neck to drink in her scent. His lips briefly touching her soft skin, his tufted goatee tickling her, bring her back to reality.

Her eyes snapped open. She jerked away from him, slapping him on the head. "Ow!"

Holly pulled her cloak tight around her neck. He looked up at her, her face turned up in disgust.

"It wasn't like that." Teniah said defensively, "I was just smelling you. No, no not creeping just …. You smelled so … good." He lowered his head and rubbed his shoulder.

"I'll give you the recipe, just don't do that again. We should get out of here. I'm not spending another night in this graveyard." She looked at Teniah and rolled her eyes. He blushed.

"Where is here exactly?" He said to Holly.

"Were still in Leto Mountains this part here is the valley. If I'm correct we should be going that way. We'll head southeast to get out of here."

The cats one by one rose to their feet from a lazy nap, missing the earlier excitement. Jetta looked at Teniah with ears half perked and purring.

4. THEN

She slept not a wink the previous night. Or the nights lead up to this. Never before had there been this much excitement in the castle. Servants bustling about their chores; cleaning every nook and cranny, rearrange anything not nailed down. Changing out old tapestries for more festive-looking ones; garlands by the dozens brought in to decorate the staircases.

Princess Holly had never seen the castle look so alive. She leaned over the railing in the east wing to smell the incense burning in the halls. The scent was so strong that she could taste it on her tongue.

Honeycomb, yum; she thought.

The ball was a week away and she wished she could go. Although she had matured into quite the young lady she knew without asking the answer would be no. She was 15 going on 16. When she turned 18, the king would hold a coming out ball in her honor but until then any party at all was forbidden. Until then she was to remain invisible, even to him.

No one knew what had come over the king. Was he in love again? Was he finally done grieving for his wife? Was he mad? Was it the Prime minister's doing to cheer up the king after years of sulking? Everyone wondered but no one knew.

What made the up-coming ball more exciting was when Princess Holly overheard nanny Noor talking to her tutoress.

"Yes Ahinoam it's perfectly true. The invitation arrived in Chriswell last week and my aunt, head-house maid to the Duke of Chriswell; overheard him say it was to be a masquerade."

"A masquerade." The slender point of Ahinoam's ears pricked up.

A masquerade, Holly echoed.

What *she* would do to go to a masquerade.

The guest had arrived a couple days before; she watched their arrival with eager anticipation. They all looked so elegant. Lords, dukes, barons, ladies, duchesses and dames. They had come from all over. Come for the ball. Servants carrying armfuls of luggage running behind them. They dined with the king and played cards every night. The guest admired the gardens outside and the conservatory inside. And gossip, always gossip. Princess Holly could hardly pay attention to her lessons; they were all having so much fun.

She had been counting down the days. She had been counting down the hours. At a masquerade she could conceal her identity and the day before she had formed the perfect disguise.

Years ago she had discovered a room while on one of her father searches. The room's once beautiful splendor had been replaced with a layer of dust and cobwebs. She figured the room must have belonged to someone special. Odd that it had been forgotten this way. While rummaging through the chest of drawers she found a Bengal tiger mask.

She wanted the mask and was certain no one would miss it. She hid it in the bottom of her own chest of drawers and had completely forgotten about it until now.

That evening as the guest dressed in their respective rooms so did Princess Holly. She ate dinner and turned in early so the servants wouldn't check on her later.

Her dress was of ivory colored tulle. It had long sleeves with finger straps and was backless. She had never worn it before; she saved it for the right occasion. She finished the outfit with layered chain necklaces and ribbons around her neck and a pearl ring with gold trimming.

Princess Holy faced the mirror.

Wow I look amazing.

But there was one thing that didn't quite fit. She looked at her face.

She was still the little girl with a wish.

But no more. Tonight she had a new wish. She didn't want to look like anyone other than herself. She had come to accept that she would not look like her mother and she could live with that.

She let her hair down and unbraided it. Fluffy it up around her face and put on the Bengal tiger mask. Her hazel eyes sparkled from behind the mask. The fiery orange from her hair and the orange in the mask gave her a mesmerizing, glowing look.

She didn't want to be the first one down. She waited in her room until she was sure the ball room would be almost full and then slip downstairs. She hid behind a pillar until other guest passed by; she walked up behind them and entered without the servants noticing her. She was one masked face among hundreds.

She didn't know any of these people. She broke away from the group and headed toward the side wall where she was not likely to draw as much attention to herself. So many people, where did they all come from? She couldn't imagine the world could hold this many.

Servants were the only ones not masked; they carried trays of fruit and cheese. Others carried drinks in tall glasses. As one servant passed in front of her he handed her a drink.

Hmm... bubbly.

The sound of trumpets, a herald and the guest parting down the middle caught the princess's attention. Men and a woman walking up the aisle were led by one man who needed no introduction; although he got one anyway.

"Announcing, His Highness Jabin the undisputed King of Avril."

Everyone bowed and curtsied as he walked by them. When he came to the end of the aisle he stepped onto the platform that held his throne. Then he turned back toward his guest and they looked expectedly at him. She saw him make a quick motion and then the music started playing. Everyone went back to mingling as before. Princess Holly stood on the very tip of her slippers to see him over the crowd, he was now sitting down. She could only see his head; he held his mask with a handle to his face but now and then he would pull it away from his face. He looked bored.

A dinner gong hummed and the masqueraders all headed to the dining hall, laughing and talking as they went. Elaborate meat and poultry dishes lined the middle of the table.

Wow this must have taken hours to put together. It looks and ....

She took a deep breath.

... Smells delicious.

Too bad she had already eaten but it was just as well. Someone was bound to start a conversation with her and they would want to know all about her. This could easily spark the attention of others at the table.

She continued walking passed the long table and all its chairs and on to the balcony. It was getting on toward dusk. She could hear everyone inside talking. The balcony was long and wrapped around the upper part of the castle. She followed it till she found a bench she could sit on.

Princess Holly didn't feel the least bit tired but wanted to lie down while she waited. After all, it would be a long dinner.

She felt good, real good. Her eyes opened, she saw featureless blackness all around her. That was normal, what wasn't normal was her bed. It felt like a hard, cold stone; short too. She was cuddled up on it like a cat taking a midmorning nap. Princess Holly yawned and stretched, she could easily have slept a few more hours. Then it clicked in her brain. She was outside.

Oh no the masquerade!

She jumped to her feet and ran for the door. Her hair flew back over her shoulders as she went. The guests were just leaving. She saw an open spot among two women and quickly slipped into it.

None of this had gone completely unnoticed. A man on the other side of the table was watching her.

The orchestra was warming up as they came in. She couldn't wait till the dancing began, she would watch it all from her claimed spot by the …

The man that had been watching her was suddenly blocking her way and appeared to be talking to her. He spoke so softly; his speech was barely audible. She didn't know what to do so she dropped him a curtsey.

"My name is Lincoln. I know it's not customary to introduce myself but after I saw you fly into the room I figure you wouldn't mind.

She said nothing.

He continued, "Perhaps you might tell me your name."

"Why not guess it?" She said slowly, unsure if she had been made.

"It would be easier if you told me."

"Yes," this time more playful, "But not as much fun." Her name was Holly, she was a princess, this was her castle, she would be the next sovereign and she was breaking *all* the rules.

"Most popular names are… Saborah, Chloe, Ardelle, Beatrice and Serena. None of them, huh? What about Pandora? Satty? Libby? Zenobia or Lacey? I give up.

"Keep going. You are getting close."

He sighed, "Kate."

"Yes." She settled on a name she could remember for the evening.

"Well Kate, I thought I knew all the beautiful ladies in Avril."

"Well I actually am not from around here."

"Then where are you from?"

"Chriswell." It was the first place to pop into her head.

"Really?"

She got the impression he was laughing silently at her.

"So am I," he said slowly.

She was thankful for the mask, her cheeks were burning. "Do you make it your business to know as you put it "all the beautiful ladies.""

"I do but clearly I missed one. I'm the Duke of Chriswell."

"You're the Duke of Chriswell?!" Of course, he would be here tonight. She wanted to slap her forehead. Nanny Noor's aunt was his head housemaid. That's why the name Chriswell was stuck in her head.

"You seem shocked. Don't I look like a Duke?"

She looked at him. He did look like a Duke. "No it's just I was expecting the Duke to be a much older man."

He smiled at her. "I'll take that as a compliment. Well, Kate of Chriswell would you care to dance with me?"

She really should have said no. A thousand reasons to say no. All of which involved him. This was probably his chance to expose her for the fraud she was. He probably hadn't figured out she was the princess, maybe just some servant sneaking in for a good time. She didn't know if that was an advantage or not.

Staring into his frost blue eyes made her skin prickle. "Yes." Somehow that was easier than saying no. "Why not, it's a ball after all."

He smiled again. He had her.

The orchestra began playing. Kate formally known as Holly, trailed along behind him as he led the way to the dance floor. She put her hand on his shoulder while he put his hand at the middle of her back. She nearly jumped; she had completely forgotten the dress was backless.

"You dance well." He said almost surprised.

She knew it; he did think she was a servant.

Through the middle of the dance she became aware that they were being watched by the king. He noticed too. He turned her around himself and looked back over his shoulder. "You have yet another admirer. Perhaps I should surrender you to him now. I could never hope to measure up to the king." He bowed.

They pulled away from the dance floor as other dancers came for the next song. "Do you know His Highness?"

She went up on her toes to see over his shoulder. He was still watching them. "Not really." She answered truthfully. She came back down "Who is that man standing near His Highness?"

Lincoln turned around; his eyes fell on a man with a swarthy complexion.

"That's Prime Minister Phalen."

"And the woman?"

"Nolee, secretary to His Highness."

She looked familiar although her face was obscured by a seaweed mask. She liked her dress, it was a seal pelt wrapped around her body.

Lincoln threw her a strange glance as though reading her thoughts. "Let's go upstairs." To the left of the ballroom was a staircase that led to a wraparound indoor balcony in which you could look down on the ballroom. He took her hand and brought her upstairs; there were people already there. Three young women were giggling as they waved to someone downstairs. One leaned over the railing and blew a kiss.

They walked around at first in silence, midway around they stopped to look at the dancers. He leaned his elbow on the railing. "It seems history is repeating itself."

"What do you mean?"

He set his eyes on her. "You're beautiful."

"How can you tell?"

"It's not that hard. Clearly I'm not the only one who thinks so." She looked form his eyes to his mask. It was bronze with a gaping, happy smile. The eye holes were like horizontal moons. It also had eyebrows shaped into it that met in the middle and connected to the nose.

"Shall I take it off for you?" He reached both hands behind his head ready to undue the straps.

"How is history repeat itself?

He lowered his hands.

'Well as the story goes, my father was in love with a Lord's daughter. They were at a masquerade ball held in honor of King Jabin who had just succeeded the throne. He saw her dancing with him and fell in love her too. The King vs. a Duke, It wasn't very hard to see why she choose the former. He could give her half his kingdom. My father settled for another noblewoman not as attractive and about a year later I was born. Years later, here I am, the new Duke of Chriswell and the same king is once again unmarried. Out of all the woman in the room, the only one he's got his eye on is the one I choose for myself. It's pretty bizarre stuff."

You're telling me! His father was in love with my mother? And my father stole her away. Why hadn't anyone told me this? She frowned at her own thoughts. She knew the answer to her own question. She didn't know this because she hardly knew anything about her parents. No one ever talked about them.

At 3am the party was staring to wind down. They had been talking on the balcony for hours, mostly about traveling and books. He asked her questions she gave him answer. Answers that were usually lies; depending on how you looked at it.

Princess Holly had never ice skated but Kate had. Princess Holly hated poems and anything that reminded her of her lessons but Kate loved poems and had even written her own.

"Wow I'd love to read yours sometime."

She laughed, "There really not that good." The thing Holly and Kate did have in common was their love for any game, particularly charades.

"It's getting late. I should go."

"Wait, when can I see you again?"

"I'm not sure. I wouldn't want to raise your hopes."

"Will you visit me at my estate if I don't see you before I leave?"

"I'll try."

"Remember its Copeland Hall in Chriswell." He called after her.

That night or rather that morning Princess Holly lay in bed trying to sleep. She heard the clock tower gong four times but she couldn't stop thinking about him. He had no idea how much history was repeating itself. His father loved her mother and he was practically in love with her. She pulled back the curtains and unlatched the window. She crawled back into bed. She wanted to watch the sun come up. As it did she wondered why she hadn't done this before.

She stared at the problem before her, Pythagorean Theorem.

$$a^2 + b^2 = c^2$$

It wasn't as much fun being Princess Holly of Avril. Not when she could be Kate of Chriswell. She was surprised she wasn't tired considering how many hours she'd been up. Thank goodness for her bench nap.

She was starting to resign herself to the fact that things were going back to the way they were. No real excitement. But she'd changed; she wasn't a person to be put off any longer. She wanted to go to Chriswell to see the Duke.

A rapping noise at the door interrupted her thoughts.

"Come in." Her tutor said in a gruff tone. A servant walked in and handed him a note. He took it and read. His eyes met hers across the room. Without a word he got up and left. She could hear voices outside the room; her tutor and someone else. She couldn't make out any words just tones that conveyed a sense of surprise.

The servant eyes were cast down; she wondered if he knew what this was all about. When he reentered the room he looked very confused saying only that she could take the rest of the day. She watched him shuffle his papers and return them to his bag.

The hallway was empty. Whoever he had been talking to was long gone. With the whole day to herself she didn't know what to do. She went to the sitting room; maybe she would play chess that always passes the time. But it was empty, the parlor too. No servants or nannies. Which was odd, there were always there. She wandered the east wing. All of the rooms empty. Finally she went to her bedroom.

There was a note propped up on her writing desk. It was an official letter, the kind the king sent. She broke open the seal and read the contents.

Her hand fell to her side. She couldn't believe what she had read.

"I'm being banished?"

She was not going to remain silent about this. She would talk to the one person who could help her, or hurt her. He was outside the King's study talking to other officials.

"What is the meaning of this?" She held up the letter for him to see.

He was writing when he glanced up from his folder. "You Highness." He bowed. "May I introduce …"

"No you may not."

He was stunned by her rude demeanor. He nodded to the others to leave them. As they walked away Princess Holly could hear them mumbling about her behavior toward them.

"You are the Prime minister, are you not?"

"Yes, Phalen Your Highness."

Princess Holly held the paper up again, closer to him. "I'm afraid I know no more about that then you." He bowed again and started to leave.

She followed at his side trying to catch his eyes but he refused to look at her. "I request a private audience with the king."

"His Excellency does not consent to your proposal."

"But you haven't even asked him."

"He told me so only this morning. He does not wish to be disturbed by anyone."

"Ask why then is he sending me away."

"I cannot do that either." He looked down at his fold, fiddling with the papers inside, trying to look busy. "I cannot interfere with His personal affairs."

"But he's my father and I'm your future queen." She grabbed his arm with both hands to keep him from leaving. She thought he would be angry that she touched him but he wasn't. His dark brown eyes reflected the distress she felt. She was a child still, a child begging not to be separated from her home. She wished in that moment he could have been her father. He didn't look like the kind of man who would send his only daughter away.

"Don't worry. Maybe the King will change his mind before you leave. All will be well." With that he pried himself from her grasp. He left her there all alone in the corridor, still holding the letter that had sealed her fate.

I am worried. History is repeating itself. The King is taking me away, far away from the Duke of Chriswell.

5. NOW

The altitude wasn't very high but Holly felt her head throb and ache, the atmospheric pressure was changing as they went down.

They were all quite; she couldn't wait to get out of there, she couldn't wait to be home.

Her ankle hurt to walk on. The makeshift bandage was holding but it needed time to heal. The worst would be if an infection set in.

When they stopped for a break Holly undressed her wound. It looked as bad as it felt. It was amazing the whole foot hadn't come off.

"That looks like it hurts a lot. No don't get up, you should rest." He looked around. "It's a shame we don't have a horse or something you could ride on. Of course, I could always carry you."

"I can manage. You have what you need anyway." She stood up. They stood inches apart from each other; she hadn't noticed the difference in their height. She wasn't use to being taller, not by much but still taller. She also couldn't help but notice his hair was a deep chestnut color that in the sunlight was irresistible to look at. "So we will be parting ways once were out of this place."

"Oh good, were back to this again. Come on, I thought we were passed all this."

"You wouldn't understand, Teniah, so let it go." She closed her eyes suddenly dizzy.

"No, not until we get this out in the open. Your father is dying, he not me wants to see you. He sent me to find you, to find medicine that only you could find."

"Anyone could have found that." She protested.

"Yes but he trusted you. He wanted you."

"He never wanted me before." She saw the expression on his face change. "I mean I wasn't the ideal child, growing up." She'd already said more than she wanted to. "You wouldn't understand."

"I would understand if you would just tell me, make me understand." He hoped her story would be quick – *I hate my father, the end* or *his castle is moldy, the end* – He didn't want to be near this place after dark again.

"I killed my mother. I'm a murderer."

"That's awful why would you do that?"

"I don't know." She turned away from him. "It was an accident, I think."

"You think it was an accident but you don't know."

She walked behind a tree and sat down. He walked around the other side to see her sitting there with her hands holding up her face. "It was so long ago." She said. "I was only a baby. I don't know why I did it."

"I am more confused now than I have ever been in my whole life."

"Just forget it."

"No, no explain it to me from the beginning and no riddles."

"I killed my mother as a baby while she was giving birth to me. Now leave me here and go."

"Holly, women die in childbirth all the time and sometimes the babies die too. It's sad but it happens. But that doesn't make you a murderer. Look I'm sure your father just wants to put the pass right. Sometimes when were near death we start to think about the ones we love the most.

She shock her head "I can't."

"Yes you can; look at me, Holly look. Yes you can. We are going back. We're going to save your father and you two will fix your problems." *The end* he thought. *The end.*

"Ok." Then she started to get up. As she did her hand pulled away from his grasp.

He thought to himself, *when had that happened?* He didn't remember taking her hand.

She didn't seem to notice.

His mind switched from one subject to another; he was not going to let her suffer in secret. He had to do something about that ankle. He waited till after they were out of the Leto Mountains, when Holly wasn't looking he gave Armin a message and sent him off; hopefully the cat understood and knew where to go. Communicating with animals was not part of his act.

He set to work making a tea from the flowers they picked, he choose the ones from his satchels.

"Here drink this."

"Where did you get the cup?" She gingerly put it to his lips. It was a tree root hallowed out and shaped into a drinking vessel.

"You don't think juggling is the only thing I'm good for? I carry my tools with me always for those middle-of-the-forest-mishaps."

"And where did you get the tea?"

"A magician never reveals his secrets." He smiled.

"Playing with coins and balls hardy qualifies you as a magician." She couldn't help mirroring that smile.

"You're right." He thought about saying something more but it was best to leave it there. He turned away from her but couldn't make himself stop smiling.

"So what's the fastest route back?" He felt more in control of his facial muscles but didn't look in her direction, just in case.

"That's easy. We continue west and cut through the Whispering Tree forest, and that will take us to Avril. From there finding the castle should be no problem. You can see the top of it for miles." Skandia came over to Holly resting her head in Holly's lap. She reached down with her free hand to pet the cat's fluffy, padded paws.

"I always wondered why they call it Whispering Trees."

"When the wind blows against the bark it sounds like the trees are talking to you. I was there once a long time ago." She wrapped her arms around Skandia and pulled her close.

He stirred the fire he had used for the tea so it wouldn't go out. Then he sat down across from her. As the fire flickered between them she was reminded of how once she thought he was strange; but now it seemed so normal, even all the hair. His personality was pleasant although he was nosey and slightly demanding.

"Teniah can I ask you a question?"

"I believe that was a question but go ahead and ask me another." He gave her a half-smile.

"Why are you here? Why did my father send you?"

"I guess that's a fair question." He thought, "He asked me to do this for him, so how could I refuse."

"But alone?"

"He said it had to be a secret. No one could know about this. He called me to his room, he had been ill for a couple days but by then he was too weak to leave his bed. He said there were those in his court that wanted a change, namely his death. With him gone and you missing, they could choose a new ruler more suited to the roll – someone they could control from behind the thrown. A puppet, if you will. He was afraid if anyone else knew they would try and stop me from coming."

"Fairytales." She exclaimed. "My father has many loyal subjects that would move earth and sky for him. He's just looking for a way to guilt me for running away all those years ago and get me killed in the process by going on a ridiculous quest."

"You can choose to believe what you like. I'm turning in now."

She looked at her ankle. A near brush with death, to get a flower that could heal her dying father because he was too lazy to send his army to get it. And then there was Teniah. He was turned away from her, sleeping on the ground. He seemed sincere enough. But this was not his fight. He was risking his life to help one stranger help another stranger.

6. THEN

She looked up at the place that would be her home until-possibly-forever. She was cold; she had ridden the entire night unaccompanied. The servants waited outside to greet her but the greeting was far from the expression of good wishes that usually connoted the term.

She had been use to a castle, the Castle; hundreds of servants. The Westwood manor house was small, the staff was small. They bowed stiffly as she passed. She was going to have to get use to a new life.

There was a letter waiting for her on the writing desk of her new bedchamber.

HOUSE RULES ARE AS FOLLOWS:

No contact is allowed with his majesty King Jabin of Avril.
No contact is allowed with anyone at court or with any servants.
No visitors are allowed.
Outings will be strictly supervised.
No outings after dusk.
No outings to the village.
No contact with the villagers of Chriswell is to be made.

By order of the King.
Signed, Prime Minister *Phalen*

Her eyes rose from the paper. She couldn't yet fully grasp what it all meant but it was to be the beginning of her isolation. She wanted to cry she didn't know which issue to cry to about. Tomorrow she would turn 16; tomorrow marked 16 years of a miserable life. Now she wondered if the next 16 would follow in suit.

Dinner that night was quiet. She sat at the head of the table hoping for noise, any noise. The footman's steps were soundless and when he sat the dishes down they didn't clink or clunk.

So bored, she thought, *so bored. If there was another person, a girl perhaps my age … yes, yes then we could talk and laugh.*

Hello Holly. Said her imaginary new friend.

Hello friend. I'll call you Kate. Fine weather where having, isn't it?

Sure we can talk about the weather, or we could play a game.

Holly lowered her fork. *A game? What sort of a game?*

This game is called look-over-your-shoulder?!

Holly froze, a fear rising up in her. She turned her head ever so slightly as she looked over her shoulder. She nearly gasped when she saw him. He was staring at her; leaning back on cabinet hutch. He had high shoulders and hardly a neck at all; he looked like a turtle retreating back into its shell.

He looked at her with a cold expression. But there was more happening behind those dark eyes; much, much more. She quickly turned back. Holly knew she hadn't been speaking out loud to herself. No, it was something else. What does he want? Why is he looking at me?

It seemed like forever with his eyes on the back of her neck. When he left, no doubt to finish other chores she left the table and went upstairs. Her appetite was gone and didn't return until morning.

She shut the door behind her and leaned back against it, not wanting anyone to enter her room. Her first night here, she was sure she wouldn't sleep. How could they expect her to stay?

She would write to the Prime Minister had she not been forbidden to. She couldn't even ask for new linen from the castle if she needed it.

Why had the king sent her here? Had she displeased him? She must have. What had she done? Nothing. She had long stopped seeking out her father for affection. Had he planned to send her away all along? Her letter of dismissal had come right after the masquerade. Is it possible he... No he couldn't have known it was her. He hadn't seen her in years and she had changed and grown so much. Besides she was wearing a mask.

She pushed herself off the door and stepped into the light of a single candle burning at her bedside table. The room was tiny compared to her previous one; although she had her own house now – which was starting to feel like a prison – none of it felt like hers. Just a tiny bedchamber; where she could be alone. Her gaze drifted from one corner to another. It wouldn't have surprised her if the whole east wing was bigger than this manor house.

She began to loosen her bodice. Her fingers stopped, a shudder past over her, her memory taking her back to a few minutes ago. The look the footmen had given her, she couldn't describe it but she didn't like it.

She looked around the room again. There was only one way to ease a troubled mind like hers. Princess Holly pulled a nightgown from her top drawer and took it over to the bed.

With one puff her breath made the room dark, and she changed where no eyes could see her.

She hated this, these so-called supervised outings. Not outing to anywhere fun. She paced back and forth in the garden. There really wasn't much to see; all the flowers had withered up in preparation for winter and wouldn't be back till next year. She looked up as she turned on the path; he was still there. He wasn't taking his eyes off of her for a second. The footmen, Neil was taking the rules a little too seriously. She didn't like the way he stared at her. It wasn't the way a gentleman ought to stare at a lady. It wasn't the way a footman should stare at a princess. It made her feel uneasy.

She felt her face going warm like it did when she blushed. Princess Holly hid her face so he couldn't see and tucked the wind-blown strands of hair behind her ear.

He was leaning against one of the pillars that supported the gazebo. Her skin crawled as she imagined him still staring; it made her feel naked. It made her feel unclean. A thousand baths could not wash the feeling he gave when he saw through her.

One of the maids joined him on the gazebo, her eyes met the princesses. Anger flickered across her face like a wavering flame from a newly lit match.

She had gone from next in line for the thrown to the value of mere peasant girl. She was out of favor with the king and they all knew it. She suspected that by now everyone had heard of her banishment. Abandoned and alone, they were taking advantage of the situation. She saw herself in their eyes: Easy prey.

She sat up in bed, batting her eyes as the light came in. A maid had pulled back the curtain. A day had turned into a week, a week into a month then six of them.

She ate alone; the cook sometimes served the food cold. The footmen only half did their jobs. The maids ignored her and only worked when they felt like it. The worst of them was Kennedi; she had a temper to match a tempest. And then there was Neil, he was the only one who liked her but for all the debased reasons. He lurked about Westwood manor house, haunting every hallway he turned down and every corridor he entered. His eyes lurked too; into every room he passed, through every window he saw. Sometimes she hid from them but she couldn't hide forever.

As head housemaid, Kennedi was supposed to dress Princess Holly but usually sent one of the other maids and usually no one came at all.

The first time Kennedi showed up to dress Princess Holly she shot her a dark look. The corset was already on when Kennedi took over to fasten it. She could feel her abdomen constrict, she squirmed uncomfortably but she only pulled harder and faster. With another rough jerk she felt compelled to cry out.

"You're pulling to hard, I can't breathe."

A sudden and sharp tug sucked the air out of Princess Holly's lungs in a manner that she knew would bruise later.

"Well I mean too." Shouted the maid close to her ear; "I'm glad too." It was almost deafening. "You hateful, wicked creature! Have you no regard for what others suffer because of you? I was well employed at the castle stables with my family." Kennedi held fast to the strings of the corset.

Holly bit back tears, screams and words not wanting it to get worse.

Kennedi only continued, "Because of you I had to leave that all behind and come here to look after the likes of you. When they all say "There goes the princess," I say "What a fancy tart she is." You're so ungrateful while others slave for you."

She tightened her grip and Holly thought her ribcage would break.

"Princess?" Kennedi snorted. "What princess are you?" Holly could feel her warm breath against her cold cheek.

Kennedi stopped her rampage and tied the knot, tight.

Was this the life her father meant for her? A life without restitution? If only he could see her now.

After a time the things that didn't interest her started to. She took more to reading, even poetry. Games weren't as fun anymore without someone to play them with. She thought a lot too. She thought about things she hadn't thought about in a while. She thought about *him*. So close but so far away. She imaged how magnificent Copeland Hall must be. Lincoln probably didn't know she was at Westwood. She had wanted to go to Chriswell, well now she was here and she still couldn't see him.

The morning that would change her life forever rolled in with a sweet fragrance. She was sitting in the window seat of her bedchamber enjoying a poem book in the quite solitude of the early morning. It was going on eight months; she was fitting in to her life the best way she knew how.

She hadn't taken her breakfast yet and the smell of incense awaked her dormant stomach from its night of fast. As she hurried to unbolt the door, she could not have foreseen what awaited her downstairs. She had started locking her door of late, a wise choice considering her living conditions.

She entered the dining room to find two of the maids talking, they both seemed like they had been crying. Almost instantly they noticed her there. One of the maids was Kennedi.

"You spy on us!" Before her tantrum could go into full effect the other maid; a horse-faced girl cut in.

"Your ladyship it's the most dreadful news. The cook is dead."

"I'm so sorry. What happened to her?"

"Like you care to know. Bet you didn't even know her name." Kennedi snapped. *She's right I don't know her name.*

"Better learn fast cause I won't feed you. And none of them neither." The maid was about to open her mouth to say something but Kennedi cut the girl a dirty look. "We all have our own work to do, not to be cookin' and haulin' for you miss royal. Get to the kitchen less you starve."

Fear moved Princess Holly's feet not to the kitchen but upstairs to the safety and security of her room and away from that woman. She nearly ran into Neil on the landing. His eyes dropped down on her and she started backing away from him. Behind her Kennedi, in front of her Neil; he stood where she need to go.

His lips parted into a smile as he anticipated her next move. It was stupid but she had to try.

She bolted. Careful not to brush against him, she went up the next flight of stairs. She thought he would grab her and drag her back down but he let her go. And go she did.

The frigid depths of winter would be here soon. She could feel the temperature slowly dropping as the evening wore on. Holly stretched her arms out over the window frame toward the moon. Beckoning it, if it would come to her, if it would fall.

What would she do? How could she go on? Her stomach jolted in her belly. She hadn't eaten since last night's super.

If only father knew what I am enduring. He would feel for me. Let me return home. No he didn't care. He sent me out to here to die.

Death by starvation. Death by cruel servants. Death by death.

"I'm sorry." A single tear rolled down her cold cheek. "So sorry." It was an accident; she never meant to kill her mother. If only he could see how sorry she was; how bad she felt.

This made her sick. The crying, thinking about her father, mother and even the servants. In all of this who was thinking about her? True, she was feeling sorry for herself already, but it was going to take a lot more than that to keep her alive.

If no one was going to feed her, she would feed herself.

If no one would let her go home, she would run away.

If no one would love her...

She got up and went to her closet, the hinges moaned as she pulled back the doors. She dressed warm, after all it was going to be a cold night.

Holly felt a lump in her throat and her eyes got watery. She was afraid to go and afraid to stay.

How will I live? I've never been on my own before. Until eight months ago I had never set foot outside the castle walls. What will my life be like now?

She stepped onto the windowsill, the cold night wind kissing her soft face as it blew pass her. She glanced back into the room as if to say goodbye to her former life. Holly climbed onto the vine growing up the side close to her window; she went down until she was close enough to the ground to jump.

She hung against the side of the house listening. The night was silent; the house staff was probably all in bed by now. She took a deep breath, and then, she bolted. Into the darkness she ran. Going in no particular direction; like a bird let out of its cage, she was free. She ran hard, she ran fast, she ran for hours with boundless energy.

Finally at dawns first light she stopped to catch her breath.

She climbed the tallest tree to check her progress. As she climbed branch by branch, the sun climbed the sky to meet her at the top. The horizon was lit and the colors were brighter than a painter's canvas. It took her breath away to see such undomesticated beauty. Valleys, mountains, streams, lakes and the endless forest that stretched off into the distance and more lay before her eyes.

She smiled; it felt like home.

As she traveled she admired her surroundings so much that hours after sun up she still hadn't eaten. Or slept. Most fruit trees were preparing for winter and had stopped producing fruit. The shrubs were bare.

What did the animals and people who didn't live in castles eat? She wondered. *Water first then I'll search for food.*

Holly went to the stream she had seen from the tree top. Holly cupped the water in her palms and sipped it. It was cool on her lips; she liked the way it rolled back over her tongue, refreshing.

She wished she had a container to collect this delicious water. But if she followed the stream she could drink whenever she felt thirsty and maybe she'd find food nearby.

As she continued she would stop to skip a rock or listen to a chirp or whistle from a bird. Birds were not meant for cages. They were not meant to depend on others for food but to catch their own. Birds were not meant to be supervised by hateful eyes or wear tight corsets for that matter. Corsets were devices of evil, constricted by evil people for the soul purpose of evil deeds. She hated corsets; and now thanks to Kennedi she'd never wear one again.

That evening she made good on her vow and roasted her corset upon the fire. The smell of burning cotton made her think of food.

If I don't figure out how to feed myself this could turn into a problem. She looked around her. *Maybe I should try grass. If the animals can eat it than how bad could it really be....*

Holly spat out the blades of grass.

Maybe not.

Day two of freedom and Holly had finally resolved her eating issue. She would eat bugs. Ants were first on the menu. Using long twig she lowered it into an ant hole and lapped up the ones that came out. Conclusion: too tedious to eat given their size and the texture was all wrong. Small things running frantic inside her mouth while she tried to chew and swallow was, well, strange.

Next she tried grasshoppers, but this time she killed them first then cooked them. The exoskeleton was crunchy, very crunchy; the inside was liquid and bland but she didn't mind. She collected more of them in the folds of her dress. It felt good to have something occupying the space in her stomach. Grasshoppers would be her food source till she could find something better.

She was doing a good job taking care of herself. Water, check. Food, check. Shelter?

Eventually it would be too cold to sleep outdoors. Most animals were preparing for hibernation in the holes of trees, a cave or underground. She would need to start preparing too.

That night she lay awake watching the fire. Figuring out fire had been easy; she had read a book about a knight-errant who built a fire by rubbing two sticks together.

She couldn't shake the feeling of being watched. It was a feeling that had been slowly growing inside her. She didn't hear anything to indicate someone was there, but in the trees who would know. She looked around her to narrow down where the feeling was coming from. Then she saw it. Dead ahead of her a pair of eyes fixed on her face. From the fire Holly could see the eyes were dazzling green.

"Who are you? Why are you hiding there?"

But the eyes made no answer.

"If you are cold, please warm yourself by the fire."

It was a little troubling and yet she was not afraid as she ought to have been. But now that she knew the eyes were there she could not ignore them.

As she debated what to do about her new guest, more eyes appeared around the forest. Some of green and blue some of blue and green. Hazel, brown and violet; all coming to watch her. She was surrounded by eyes.

The green eyes came toward her from the deep cover of night. This Nork must have been crawling for the eyes were lower to the ground.

As the eyes continued slowly a silhouette took shape, the form was unmistakable in the fire's glow. Holly bit the back of her hand to silencing a scream. It was a caracal. The cat showed no fear of her or the fire. The other eyes came into the light as well.

The female cat met her face-to-face. It's radiant, pulsing eyes seem to ease her troubled mind. A low humming from the cat's chest made her realize, that this animal meant her no harm. Staring into the caracal's eyes made her dizzy, filled her mind with words, names, places. "Eu-RE-Ka." She looked at the tufted hair at the tip of the cat's ears and tawny fur. She was shocked at her own words. "Your name is Eureka."

A bobcat leaped forward and skidded to Eureka's side. The wild cat eager for an introduction could easily have torn her into bit size chunks. She admired the ruffs of extended hair beneath the ears almost like a mutton chop beard. His name was Lafayette. She wanted to pet his soft facial hair but dared not.

One brushed passed her, she jerked away from it. He stopped a couple feet from her, holding his tail high and looked back. He seemed to be saying: *Allow me to introduce myself. They call me Cody, I'm a cheetah.*

Holly could feel a rumbling purr; the sensation was followed by a kneading from small paws on her lap. A Rusty spotted cat stood there waiting to be noticed. The cat meowed out her name. My name is Tess, but you can call me Tess.

One by one the cats were coming in closer, attack formation. Surrounded by the enemy, except they weren't the enemy. If a wild animal didn't attack a would-be forest wanderer then they simply ignored they presence and stayed away. Was there something special about her?

A tiger pushed passed Cody. His golden eyes looked her up and down then focused on her face. Letters appeared in her mind, scrabbled like a puzzle then organized itself to form, a name. The first letter was a C, the second H, then A and D.

Chad?

She would have reckoned something far worse coming from a creature his size; like perhaps an invitation to become his next meal. Instead, he was giving her his name, she felt compelled to speak to this cat.

"It's a pleasure to meet you Chad, I am Prin... my name is Holly." She corrected herself, not a princess anymore. But Chad seemed so incurious about her name and background. The realization sparked. They already knew her or at least knew what they wanted to know about her without her ever saying.

The runaway, the outcast in need of help, so much help. Here they all were to offer her aid, with their varying talents and abilities; they could teach her all they knew. They could help her.

What a curious brunch they were. A family pack made up of the most dangerous killers of the feline ranks.

And now her.

They were extending a unique invitation, rarely given in the inhospitable wild.

Join us

The temperature was dropping. The cold air prickled the back of her neck. The break between the hot sun and the cold snow was the longest season of all. Waiting for the first snowflake to fall; it would fall but when? She could fall asleep one night and wake up under a blanket of snow.

One of the cats dropped a red stag at her feet. That was a lot of meat; they would need such kills to keep them warm and fat. Poor thing she thought.

The cat eyed her, no doubt sensing her remorse. She had met him along with the others last night, his name was Tor. This cat's genus was known by many different names; cougar, mountain lion, catamount, But it preferred to be known as a puma.

There were so many of them to remember. Alexia was the fishing cat. She was distinguishable by the slight webbing on her feet, good for swimming. Frost, a white tiger; a tiger like his cousin Chad. The bright turquoise of his eyes with the combo of white fur stripped black made him quite fetching. Y'Vonne, the Ocelot. Had two black stripes line both sides of the face, and the long tail is banded by black. Lear, the ... what was Lear? That's right a panther. He matched well with the night. There was even a Tiglon, a unique hybrid. Junius was almost all white with amber strips.

Leopold, Gig and Eden. Leopold the leopard's head, lower limbs and belly are spotted with solid black, easy enough to remember. The other two were tricky. Gigi, she bit lip trying to recall which one she was. Perhaps the one with the long bushy tail. The marbled cat. Then Eden must be the Jaguar. She was a fun cat to look at, large spots with small spots inside. Martha the margay had dark brown rosettes. Ziba was a serval; her large ears gave away her species. But those ears had helped them hunt; she could listen for the slightest movement of prey.

Just then Mac an Amur leopard came to her, looking up at the sky. He sat back on his hind legs for a better view. Holly followed his gaze. The first snowflake, a single one fell from the sky then more and more. His thick coat of spot-covered fur this would keep him warm.

A day before they came to The Whispering Tree forest Percy a pumapard, a blend of a puma and a leopard he had stretched his dwarf body over a big boulder. As she prepared a new fire, he told her in short that the Whispering tree forest was known to make those who enter it feel like they were going crazy. Good thing he warned her, the wind blowing against the bark really was maddening.

Holly pulled the moose skin tighter around her body. It wasn't the cold that chilled her but the voices. They said things but not things that made since. Just whispers, behind her, in front of her, and from side to side. Two of the cats stayed close to her, reassuring her. She was safe. Addy a snow leopard with smoky gray and whitish under parts almost fooled Holly into thinking she was alone until she caressed the back of Holly's hand with short muzzle.

The cats didn't seem bothered by it. There was something magical about the scenery. The sun was so bright, it cut into her eyes but it made each flake on the tree branches sparkle like mini rainbow.

She was sorry to leave and glad she couldn't stay.

Holly's tongue moved over her teeth searching for the dry-rub meat caught there. Meanwhile her eyes followed a red squirrel as he scurried from one branch to another, then to a hollowed out part of the tree where it disappeared into the warmth of its layer.

The worst of winter was coming.

The castle stood out, gray and sodded against the background of the snow-clad mountains. It was best structure they had found. By best it was: Crumbling from tower to tower; slanted porch and pillars and a large staircase sinking on its foundation.

Bret, Blair and Marla were the first to check it out. Holly followed behind Blair's near-black, melanistic tail as it swayed back and forth. The black Jaguar's barely visible spots disappeared as the darkness engulfed them.

The room was enormous; it had a long hallway with two rows of pillars on either side. She passed several paintings of rose gardens covered in dust. The hallway ended at a platform with a wall of glazed blue bricks in the background. On the platform was a broken long-back chair. It was clear this place had not been inhabited for some time; but it must have been beautiful to see.

Blair sniffed the bricks, Holly watched her pace the wall.

There was something there.

"What is it?"

Blair reached up and pawed one of the bricks till at last it gave way. A secret door popped open, it was filled with documents, and some looked ready to crumble if touched.

Bret and Marla were already exploring the rest of the castle. Staircases that lead nowhere, rooms that were barren, chandeliers lowered to the ground.

Blair and Holly stayed motionless for a while, just staring at the decay of what had once been.

Sleeper's door

"Huh?" Holly bent down to be at the cat's eyes level. She sniffed the air, smelling the stories of long ago.

Sleeper's door castle

"Is that what this place is? What happened to them?"
Local superstitions. Rats.
Bret joined them. He was a Jaguarundi (Eyra cat) with short legs, an elongated body and a coat like that of fox.

Plague.

"Plague."

Eviction.... bills

Marla chimed in.
"Summer castle; poorly constructed." Holly added. The predecessors never stood a chance. She could fell the wind even now, it rattled through the walls.
Marla touched noses with Blair, smelling each other; it was a form of communication Holly was still adjusting to. She caught a few words from the clouded leopard. Then she left; when she returned the other cats came too. Marla knew Holly couldn't see well. She picked up one of the sticks protruding from the bon fire outside and brought it in. Marla's fire lit up her ochreous ground-colored fur that was obliterated by dark, dusky-grey blotched patterns.
Then Holly understood what she was saying, the castle would do for now.
They wintered there.

7. NOW

Holly slept with Tibet curled in her lap, propped up against a boulder. When her eyes opened she was surprised not to see faded walls and icy landscapes.

"Dreaming of better times?" Teniah asked.

She smiled at him weakly. "Well of colder times. Armin. Armin?"

"I sent him …" A lump settling in his throat, his words caught and would not come up. The coughing was helping but not by much. "… Sent him out."

"Out where? Why? Oz, what's happening?" The Lion was at her side in a flash; licking her face with his thick pink tongue.

"I'm not sick." She said to Teniah. "It's really not that bad. I don't need help"

"Did the kitty tell you that?"

"His name is Oz. And yes."

"You're pale, beyond pale." He cocked his head, squinting. "You're practically see-through." There was a long pause between the exchange. Tibet stretched on Holly's lap distracting her momentarily. He had switched places with Skandia.

"It's for the best, Holly. It's for the best."

He wanted only the big ones but they all came. Holly was hurt; they needed to be there for her. She was like one of them. He choose five of the strongest; Junius, Tor, Percy Leopold and Cody to pull Holly. He didn't think of them as having smarts but they were one step ahead of him. Eden and Frost pulled a sled with their mouths for Holly to lie on.

The fever made her body quake. Holly was barely able to stand, she leaned her weight on Lear and Mac. They all took turns helping her in some way, even Jetta, for the first time left his side to help. Once situated Skandia and Tess laid on her to keep her warm.

Marla, Blair and Alexia led the procession all the way back to Avril. Lafayette, Gigi, Bret and Y'Vonne were at the rear guard. It felt like a military marching through the words.

No predator would dare come near them now.

Holly's fever was touch and go. He kept her talking most of the time.

"So why do you have so many cats?"

"I don't have them, they have me. Without them I would have never have made it through the winter. The Whispering Trees is a bewitching wilderness for sentimentalist of all ages but the winter there is treacherous."

"So your there Nork, touching. But you take care of them now and they live with you."

"We stumbled across Sleeper's door castle and stayed for the winter but by spring we were all fond of the place and well, never left. There independent, cats are more resourceful than humans. There not pets their friends."

"But they listen to you." He insisted.

"I listen to them too."

"You give them names."

She laughed, "They gave themselves those names."

He shook his head. He didn't understand how it was with them. He looked from

Oz to Armin; the lion's mane was as blond as the rest of his body, with the typical tufted tail. Armin, the liger was significantly bigger; he had a lionesque tawny background with faint rosette markings.

"Tell me more about yourself." She switched subjects.

"There's really not much to tell."

"Well you're close to the king, start there."

"My job brings me in line with a lot of nobles. Working at the castle is the best gig ever though. I guess I've always enjoyed entertaining people."

"It must be fun."

It was, but now there was nothing left to say. The cats seem to be taking turns hunting and well, leaking. A group of four or more disappeared then reappeared only for another group to go missing. He broke the awkward silence with, "We should rest here. Maybe you could tell them to stop."

They halted almost immediately, "I think they understood."

"Well, let's take a look at your ankle." He undid the wrapping slowly and carefully. The skin around the wound looked dead, it was gray and wrinkled. Part of the skin had been torn away, the rest ley back like a flap from a purse, pulled back to reveal the fleshy inside.

The smell reached Holly, she wanted to gag. Teniah put the leaves and petals from the tea around her wound and redressed it with a fresh bandage ripped from her cloak.

"You have many talents. Tell me, what else can you do." She said as he finished.

"Just the basics; things you learn when you have to live on your own. I expect you know a little of that. And don't worry there's plenty of these left for the king as well."

She slept the rest of the way back. Even though she could feel the sun's rays on her skin she still felt cold. The off and on tingling sensation under the bandage would bring her out of sleep briefly. She wondered if that meant it was working. It hurt less, way less. In fact, she flexed her foot then rotated her ankle clockwise, then back counter clockwise. Actually, it didn't hurt at all.

The sled started slowing down until it came to a complete stop. She arched her neck to see behind her. She could see Teniah, he was staring at something. She couldn't see passed him from that position but she felt she already knew what it was.

She pulled herself up and turned around. The honeycomb pillars, octagon shaped windows, and the long wall keeping those undesirable out and those needed in. It seemed to Holly she was dreaming; even as a soft rain fell dampening her hair, it was too surreal for her to take in.

She passed him, getting closer and closer to the place of her youth. She was placid, coming to terms with it. She was accepting it. She was waiting for it. She was ready for it.

Suddenly Holly's knees buckled, her eyes shut. Martha and Addy rushed to her side with him in tow. Teniah wiped wet blades of grass and dirt off of her check.

It was too much for her but it wasn't the fever that brought it on. The fever had broken; she had made it through just fine.

Almost fine.

She looked peaceful, no longer conscious of the world around her. Things would be better once she got to see her father. They would reconcile and all would be as it should.

One of these day's she'd thank him for all of this.

8. THEN

It was Ziba who had alerted her to his presence in the castle. The cat knew her sense sharp. The doors were not locked, they were never locked. With a Pride like theirs who had they to fear.

Ziba's head tilted, listening to a noise Holly could not hear. Holly was wearing a cream-colored dress with soft gray trimmings and spaghetti straps and a butterfly pendent attached at the base. A dragonfly necklace hung around her neck, no shoes. Everything faded and worn, all the remains of a once regal princess, unrecognizable from the years she'd grown and been away.

His face was unfamiliar, his voice a whisper like the wind. He was searching for someone; Princess Holly of Avril.

Who was that? It had been so long since she heard her name spoken; three years maybe more, she couldn't remember.

It was then that he saw the cats come into the light from the darkest corners of the castle. Chad sniffed in his direction, picking up smells of far and unfamiliar places.

"No one by that name, or that title lives here. What do you want with her?"

"I have a message for her." His voice broke at the last word.

"I will hear what message you have and convey it as I see fit."

"I would much rather to give it to her directly." He didn't seem to be fooled by lies. "She is a friend of mine."

"Very well Princess. Your father is dying."

Father. She hadn't spared a thought for him. She had left behind that life, that world and had never dreamed of going back.

The past rushing in on her was too much. What if she went back and he banished her again? Back to the nightmare she left. Now he's dying and she's needed. Her head would burst!

She kicked him out unceremoniously. Then worse let him back in. But no time for regret she was off to save her father come what may.

9. NOW

It had all been a terrible nightmare for a scared 8 year old girl but it was over now. She was safe in her room, tucked in her bed, safe. She had imagined herself dying, trying to save her father also dying. There were cats, lots and lots of cats and someone named Teniah. Impossible! She had never left. She had never been banished, never runaway.

There was however, something bothering her. Chewing at the edge of her mind; all was not well. She flung herself from the bed and rushed to meet her mirror.

Can't be!

What she saw took her breath away. The reflection of her didn't match what she had expected to find. She almost didn't recognize herself; it was her but older, taller.

Then it was all real.

The strangeness of being back at Avril had temporally caused her to forget her life in the common world. She was not sorry in the least; she had a life of her own and a home to go back to. She had friends. Now she needed to find them.

Teniah jumped to his feet at the sound of the door being yanked open. He had been sleeping in a chair, not comfortably.

"Where have they gone?"

"Holly you're looking much rejuvenated. I trust you slept well?" He sounded relived.

"How long have I been here?"

"A couple hours, maybe more. Wait!" He called after her as she hurried down the hallway. "Don't you want to change?" Holly opened a door, stuck her head in then slammed it shut. Then she looked in another one but didn't find what she was looking for. "Or perhaps put on a robe?"

"Where is she?" She faced him with her arms folded across her chest like she was ready to fight.

"Who are we talking about?"

"Skandia and the others, where are they?"

"Well, you see it's kind of hard to explain. Not everybody shares your love for fluffy, large felines. They have what you might call a "No lethal cat policy". You had what fifty of them?"

"Twenty-seven."

Well, they confiscated your twenty- seven."

"What do you mean *confiscated?* Teniah tell me where they are."

"What was I to do? Through myself down in front of the guards and there pointy swords and say 'Please don't take the big scary kitties'."

"There not scary. There my friends."

"So you've said."

A servant materialized out of nowhere, he bowed. "The king will see you as soon as you can make yourself..." He eyed the gold trimmed nightgown, "... decent."

There was an air of emptiness about this part of the castle. Off and on she had pondered Teniah's words: *He said there were those in his court who wanted a change. A ruler more suited to the roll.*

Could that be true?

Banisters draped in black, white roses in vases decked each hall, servants with black arm patches. They were already in morning for him.

She had chosen the only dress in her closet that could still fit. It was white with lace sleeves, cream colored ribbon wrapped around the waist. A flower charm jingled at her wrist. She hoped it was *decent*.

The bedchamber was guarded by two soldiers. They parted as she approached. The glided-gold knob teased her; the promise of redemption, perhaps just beyond the door. Teniah had gotten her this far, could she make it the rest?

The guards apparently noticing her uncomfortable hesitation left her alone; with her thoughts.

Her stomach was agitated, her lips quivered. The room was dark expect for a single candle at the bedside table, illuminating his pale, sickly face. Once he was thought to be the most handsome man in the entire kingdom, now he was bald and his eyes faded to grey. He did not; in anyway resemble the man she once knew.

Over the years she was away she'd changed but never thought he would. She stopped short, almost froze to the floorboards she could not move. His gaze was fixed on Holly but she didn't approach until he beckoned.

"Come closer child."

She bowed to him, "Your Highness has sent for me."

"And you came."

"And I came." She affirmed.

"You should not have bothered. Was it you aim to injury me further? To remind me of the life I lost."

"You will get better. You still have a life."

"Not the one I want."

"I don't understand. I never tried to hurt you father; only to have the one thing you denied me my whole life."

His eyes studied her face, searching for the answer.

"Your love." Holly spoke at last. "The guidance and discipline that comes with that love."

"I did not give you my love because I do not love you. Never loved you. Never wanted you." He looked pensively into the distance. "I loved her. I would give her anything she requested. She wanted you. But our lives were already perfect."

"I am sorry. I have been sorry."

"You took her from me."

"I didn't mean to."

"How could I forgive you, love you, when you were the reason the love was gone."

Tears threaten to leave her face and roll down her check. But he was not finished, yet.

"Then you showed your disrespect for me and contempt for your people by deserting your right as my heir for the throne."

"You banished me! Sent me away packing." The tears she had held back for years slipped out of her control. Angry, fear, sadness and confusion mixed with the salty water. All hope of them making peace and putting the past behind them was shattered.

I never loved you.

She had allowed Teniah to raise her hopes only so they could come crashing down at his hands. "Where did you send me? Who did you send me with? To a place as cold as yourself; with no allies. No one to protect me, no one to talk to."

"I had to send you away." He snapped. "You looked like her so much I, I couldn't even look on you. Never more so until that night; at the masquerade. The shock I endured binds me still. To see my Teresa, very much alive dancing. Dancing with the Duke of Chriswell. Just like she did when first I loved her and knew she was the one for me. And now to see her again after all these years…" He paused collecting himself; he was dying but he still had his pride. He wouldn't cry in front of her. "… Even her mask you wore. How could you be so cruel? When I was able to reason with myself that it was only you, it was like you killed her again."

He knew. She had told herself that he wouldn't have, couldn't have known. Her disguise had fooled the servants, but not the one it should have fooled. It had only made clear her true identity. All these years she could not shake that burning questioned of what had prompted him to send her away. Now, at last she knew.

Her eyes burned. Her heart burned. *I never loved you.* She had bared her soul. *You denied me of what I wanted most. Your love.* He had flung it all back in her face. *I never loved you.*

"Leave me now. I don't wish to see your face again. The tea should have finished boiling by now. Once I am made better by that power, you will return to Westwood, the manor house you so despise and wait for me to send for you."

As she reached the door he mumbled under his breath, "If I send for you." It was that last indignity that made her wild.

She wandered, though not knowing where. To the kitchen, though not knowing why. The bitter exchange left her with a red in her eyes she could not shake. She was called back to reality, and the reality was this: She wasn't noticeable, she wasn't lovable and she was completely expendable.

The cook and kitchen maid looked curious, "Isn't that…" The words faded on the air.

The kitchen was large but most of it shrouded with only a few candles to light the woman's work.

Holly's attention was caught by a small kettle whistling on the stove. She watched the kitchen maid take a silver-plated podstakannik down from the cabinet. The hot liquid poured out into the podstakannik drinking glass was almost hypnotic.

La fleur de nuit, for her, had been for naught.

"Would you like to bring the tea to the king yourself?" Her soft voice and kind eyes were lost on Holly. She reached for the podstakannik mechanically and turned around. Instead of going to the door she went to the sink in the back of the kitchen. Her vision blurred like a fog consuming the world around her. The chipping and chattering of the woman over mundane things got further and further away till they were barely audible. She lifted it and tilted it over the sink. It spilled out of the podstakannik until only a cream-colored drop remained on the rim.

She fled before first light, guided by her senses through the dark. Her feet picking up speed with every step. Tripping and falling. Stumbling and crawling. Her body dead with exhaustion but she pushed herself on.

She carried with her the secret into the night. But the secret would soon be discovered, and then the whole kingdom would be up and arms. Holly could picture herself being dragged through the streets, trying desperately to kick herself free from hoards of His Majesty's subjects.

They could choose a ruler more suited to the role; someone they could control. With the king dead and a murderous princess, they could do exactly that.

Murderess? Her? Pour the tea. She has poured the tea. Years of playing a murderer had blurred the lines to her becoming one. Holly hadn't gone there to kill her father but she just couldn't help herself, stop herself. Just like before.

Now orphaned having killed both parents, she accepted her lot in life and she contemplated what to do. Roam the countryside alone again? A chill in the air made her halt. Winter would be here in a few months. Like an animal of the world she knew planning ahead was key. The long autumn afforded her that opportunity. How did she make it on her own all those years ago?

Time had eased some memories.

10. THERE

His hooves lightly clicked across the marbled floor. It seemed like decades since he had been here. Creaks in the sealing he hadn't noticed on his first visit, made him feel they had been away longer.

This was the last place she'd go. He knew that. Still he came anyway. Maybe there was a clue. He remembered her standing there, in the throne room. He expected someone brackish or perhaps delicate in health but not at all what he found. Brave, beautiful, guileless; although not bedecked in the manner of those born into the royal line, she was radiant.

His thought of her diminished as he climbed the stairs. Each creak in the floorboards unsettling him in such an empty; cold place.

He came to the first floor, rows of rooms on each wall. If he had been Holly which room would he have slept in? The room's closet to the stairs would have been too drafty. But he was convinced she wouldn't have slept in the ones at the other end either. The long hallway stretched so far back, the light couldn't reach it. In the dark, she would have felt isolated. The middle was a good place to start.

The door was unlocked, it revealed a tidy bedchamber. Willowy, white canopy hanging from an oak bedframe with oversized floral throw pillows across the white, quilted comforter. Teniah was about to shut the room when noticed a slumped figure in the window seat. It was a woman, her head was turned away. The weak posture, faded hair and tattered clothing belonged to someone who had aged from a hard journey.

Holly? It couldn't be.

Plumes of grey smoke escaped the fireplace in the chilly bedroom. This was the last place anyone would look for her. The woods had carefully hidden her away once and they could do so again.

Sun-dried figs were the only edible things in the kitchen. She ate them hungrily. Holly remembered the summer they picked these. A picture superimposed itself over the bleak white walls of a time, and where she could be happy. Of mountains and trees and shimmering fruit. She could see them all; frocking through the underbrush. All those months of meat left her body starving for fruit. She picked far more than she could eat in one setting and saved them for another time. She had such fond memories of all her friends.

The picture faded into the bleak world that was now hers and hers alone. Holly rested her head for what seemed like a moment against her knees; time slipped away from her and she was not conscious of the day or night. She tried to conjure up more of those happy times.

Something woke her from her sleep. A voice, she heard, her name, someone calling to her in the distance. Bring her back, back to now.

"What are you doing here? How did you find me?" She growled at a figure all too familiar to her.

"I came to find you. It also wasn't very hard." Her coldness hadn't dimmed Teniah.

His brows were furrowed as he studied her face, searching for something. She didn't know what. "You look thirsty. Shall I fetch you some water?" He gestured toward the door he'd come from. She was about to dismiss him when she noticed him shifting his weight from one hoof to the other.

The setting seemed familiar. Hadn't they done this before? She had hid away, shut the world out. He had found her, brought her back. The present was plagiarizing the past. They had come full circle. Were they destined to do this again and again?

Not if she had anything to say about it.

"Go away Teniah? You already know what I'm capable of. Now leave."

"What you're capable of. What would that be? He moved toward her, a curious look in his eyes. He seated himself in a small part of the window seat she wasn't occupying. Holly was silent and remained so, for she couldn't force the words out.

"What happens now? Where do you go from here?"

"It's clear I can't stay here. Who knows who else will wander by. The whole kingdom will descend on me before a fortnight passes. Maybe I'll go south; I've never gone far south before."

"And the thrown? Your next on line; Will you forsake your duty once again?"

"What duty? I have no duty to them or you or anybody else. The thrown can sink or float, I won't be there. There will be no Holly. There will be no maiden of Avril."

"Is that all you have to say to me."

"On that subject and any other, yes."

"Holly. He's not dead. The king lives still." Their eyes met. "Your father is alive. I confess it now, to you and these walls, to bear witness to how blind I have been. I followed you to the king's bedchambers. My curiosity has always done me more harm than good but at last it seems to have paid off.

The relief that swept over her was unimaginable and drained all strength from her body and left her light-headed and gasping like a half-drowned swimmer. Her heart rate gradually returned to normal.

He continued explaining keeping in mind she was a fragile mess. "I had expected a reward, gratitude, an acknowledgement for all your hard work. You were right about him and I steered you right back to him. I was ready to kill him myself; it wasn't hard for me to imagine how you were feeling.

I crept down into the kitchen and changed out the teas when no one was looking and sent it to him by way of the footmen.

"You saved me from a fate worse than death." She looked like she was ready to cry, but her eyes remained surprisingly dry. "Thank you."

"Well princess, now that you know the truth perhaps you'll reconsider staying."

"Perhaps… but I'm no princess."

"Yes you are." A smile spreading from cheek to cheek; "You don't need Avril. You are a princess and this is your castle. The surrounding, untamed wilderness your kingdom. You have plenty of feline camaraderie's and me; if you want me. I am available for hire, as I am now unemployed. My reference and resume can be summed up this:

He took out the glass orb, precariously balanced it on the tips of his fingers then dropped it to one palm and did a palm-to-palm transfer, then back up to the starting position. He kept it going and the motion reminded her of a Venus fly trap. Teniah brought it back to the palm of his hand and moved it around one hand, then around the other. The orb seemed suspended as he moved his hands over it. He continued with embellishments, moving it down his arms and rolling it around his wrists.

She smiled watching the orb pick up his reflection in the light coming through the window.

"There is a surprise waiting outside."

"A surprise?" A faint color lit her cheeks as she bit her lip trying to bite back an excitement she could not suppress.

She followed his lead; down the staircase she'd walked so many times. He pulled back the two heavy oak doors letting the bright sunlight in. As her eyes adjusted she could make out only the silhouette of crouching figures; then finally her vision became clear and she could see. The lustrous manes catching the light made almost a halo glow; the tawny, speckled, spots and strips of the others. They were all here!

Skandia stepped forward carrying in her mouth a garlandlike writhe of flowers, leaves and berries intertwined and streaming off it.

She placed it in Teniah's open palms. "For you my Lady, no princess is complete without her crown. Ladies and Gentlemen or felines of all breads, I give you Her Highness, Princess Holly of Sleeper's door. They bowed to her: Eureka, Oz, Leopold, and Armin, all of them bowed.

Teniah went to Skandia's side; he made a one knee bow while resting his arms on the unbent one.

Although it was time for the sun to rest on the horizon it seemed to not want to set. But maybe it was her and not the sun that wasn't ready to set. She felt radiant, twin in power to it. The echo of cheers leapt up, far into the air and on into the night.

Once upon a time there was a princess who had everything materiality but lacked a warm, happy family. An outcast from her home and former life, she escaped a world of cold retribution. At first a wandering recluse then befriends the most cunning and feared cats, who are enchanted by her innocence and melancholy. They become castle dwellers but her former life hung over her still until the night that changed it all.

She answers the call of a stranger to save her father. But after all is said and done, her father shows his true and ungrateful self. Finally able to let go of the past she finds a place she really belongs and those she really belongs with.

As I unwind the memory of that time I hear the ones I love calling me; back to someplace I want to be. There is already enough pain in this world and I don't want to add to it. That's why I write it here; so I can't take it with me. So I can't hold on.

But I won't stay here writing about this sadness, I know I will put down this quill and join those who are my family now.

And WE lived happily ever after.

THE END.

WORD GLOSSARY

Nork: A fictional race of creatures that vary in appearance, size, shape and characteristics.

Leto: A fictional mountain where La fleur de nuit grows. The name Leto is taken from the fictional character in Greek mythology. Daughter of Coeus and Phoebe, mother of Apollo and Artemis by Zeus.

La fleur de nuit: a fictional flower that blooms only at night and is known for its beauty and healing properties.

Rosettes: a structure or color marking on an animal suggestive of a rosette; especially: one of the groups of spots on a leopard.

Melanistic: 1: an increased amount of black or nearly black pigmentation (as of skin, feathers, or hair) of an individual or kind of organism.

2: intense human pigmentation of the skin, eyes, and hair

Ochreous: 1: an earthly usually red or yellow and often impure iron ore used as a pigment.

2: the color of ocher; especially: the color of yellow ocher.

Lionesque: Having the characteristics of a lion.

EGG STEALERS
A short story

"What are you afraid of, a fate worse than death?" whispered Shay.

"No just death, isn't that enough?" I whispered back. I stepped one foot inside the cave and froze as a sheet of suffocating rain hit me. I was certain the beast would wake with so much noise but it slept on. If I woke the Dragon before I could get close enough to steal the egg it would probably eat me. I reminded myself this was my idea.

Back Touchstone village the task didn't seem so daunting; in fact boredom was the real issue. I wasn't bored anymore. Bedsides, who's going be more popular than the guy who swiped a dragon's egg right from under her nose? So here I was about to seal my fate.

I continued my slow-motion course with clench teeth and sweaty fits. As I advanced, the air from the Dragon's nostrils nearly knocked me over but I gained my balance. I looked back at Shay who remained at the mouth of the cave. He pretended to wiped sweat from his brow in a sign of relief. I turned back, I was now close enough to reach out and touch her. Just beyond her was the egg; in a nest of tattered clothes, bones, hair, sticks, leaves and pebbles. I eased myself into the nest being careful the whole time not to make much noise. The egg was as big as I was and about as heavy. I wrapped both arms around the biggest part of the egg and pulled it up. Now all I had to do was back my way out.

First the nest; tricky, I was almost to the rim when I looked up to see its eyes peal open. I froze. Could it see me? I got my answer a second later; it growled and slowly rose to her feet. She was very big, and tall, and very angry. I really can't imagine why.

Oh wait, I was holding her egg. The only way out was currently being blocked by a not-so-jolly-dragon. Now I'd like to take a minute to say my life fleshed before my eyes but it really didn't.

Time and everything around me seem to be moving very slowly; I was staring death in the face and it stared back, ready to burn me to a crisp.

She opened her mouth.

I opened mine, trying to scream; as though screaming might just save me. It was worth a try.

Then, Shay was at my side, pushing me out of the way of the fireball heading straight for me. We fell back, hitting the cave floor pretty hard. "Run!" He shouted Shay grabbed me by my shirt and pulled me to my feet. We tore out of there, running through dragon legs.

We were out of the cave before she realized she missed us. Something loud crackled overhead like thunder, looking over my shoulder I could see the noise was coming from her. She ran after us.

"Hey it stopped raining." I mentioned.

"Uh angry, mother Dragon chasing us; might want to focus."

There was a lake at the bottom of the mountain; we were heading straight for it. While I was thinking and not looking I tripped over a stone, fell, slid on loose dirt the rest of the way down. Also I crashed into Shay who slid down with me. The steep slope was bumpy. I could feel my trouser pants ripping; my bare knees getting cut up. As we neared the slope's end we tumbled to an abrupt stop with a hard bang. That same loud noise descended upon us followed by a large flapping sound that change the direction of the wind. I jumped up and ran for the lake with Shay in tow.

I splashed out into the deep part but sank before I could so much as take breath.

The weight of the egg dragged me down (I didn't realize I was still carrying it). A dark shadow passed overhead that caught my attention, and for a second it took my mind off drowning. I felt a tug on my leg; Shay was pointing up for us to surface. Together we swim with the egg to the top. Air never felt so good in my lungs.

"Thou hast done well!" A congratulation and a pat on the back waited for me on the bank. Shay smiled. My body was starting to ache. Aside from scraped shins and forearms and cut knuckles; there was nothing much wrong with me.

"Well, we better get back I think. She'll be back. And when she does we don't want to be here." I noticed a small crack at the top of the egg as we walked. Either it was breaking from me falling or it was hatching.

Which also meant depending on how far along it was; we'd be having either scrambled or roast dragon.

Shay carried the egg the rest of the journey back to the village. His mother was at the gate waiting. She gave Shay a slap on the back of the head, "So you finally decided to come back? I didn't believe your father when he tol' me. I say, 'My son catching dragon eggs. My son brings back the whole dragon.'" She shook her head. Then she turned her attention to me. She gave me a kiss on each cheek. "Albi, How you get so dirty, huh? How you get so dirty?" She dusted dirt from my hair. Finally, she left taking the egg on a wheelbarrow.

Once we were alone again Shay teased me by licking his fingers and wiping my face, mimicking his mother's course tone of voice. "How you get so dirty Albi?" I shoved him, but I was no match. He responded by putting me in a headlock.

I saw a figure coming toward us and Shay saw it and stopped wrestling. At first I thought it was his mother again but as he released my head I could see it was Donna. I was going to say hi when a sharp pain cut me off and I collapsed to my knees. Shay had planted an elbow in my ribs.

Donna was a small pixie-like creature, next to Shay she looked like a child. Shay never talked about her, at least not to me. I decided it was best to leave those two alone to talk in hushed tones. As I made my way to my house, I thought about how nice it would be to lay down, shut my eyes and forget this day ever happened. I pictured dad in his chair getting a fire start for the evening. Before I could make it all the way home however, Merrill the weaver's son caught up with me. He was particularly excited about our little escapade and wanted to hear the story, uncensored. I gave him a play-by-play but I was too exhausted to dramatize it.

"Well I want in. I know where we can find more eggs. We should go again tonight."

Tonight? I thought. I want to go to bed. Sleeping is what I'll be doing tonight.

"I can hardly wait." Said Merrill; an intense excitement growing behind his eyes. "It's about time we show those lily-lizards whose boss."

"You do realize were not slaying any of them." I pointed out

Dad was napping in front of the fire when I came in. It seemed a shame to wake him and it was the excuse I needed to get rid of Merrill.

I got a chance to clean up, tend to my wounds and change into something decent. I was just about to hit the sack when a heard a faint tap at the door. I answered it ready to shoo whoever it was away. "Shay?" I figured he would be resting. Merrill was standing behind him grinning and waving at me.

"Merrill and I are going to swipe some more eggs. Come with us. Oh come on you're the expert!"

So here I am, once again. Idiot! Correct me if I'm wrong, but wasn't a certain someone all giddy about showing them whose boss? Yet I'm the one sneaking into the cave, passing another dragon to grab yet another egg. You would think since I did this earlier today I wouldn't be so nervous. But I was trembling involuntarily. If that's not nervous then tell what is. A fate worse than death; or just death, or just fate. I inched around the dragon's body quietly but perhaps to close and woke it. Its red eyes snapped open and fixed on me. It gave a low growl.

Here we go again.

The End!

A COLLECTION OF POEMS

A MARTIAN WRITES HOME

Dear Family

I'm sure you wonder, since coming to earth, what I've done with my life.

I'm proud to tell you, I met a beautiful blonde and asked her to be my wife.

On earth I've become a citizen and now pay the tax.

It's quite an honor I think to be able to give something back

The system is quiet lovely but not all seem to get it

If you run a red light the police kindly remind you to quit it

People are so healthy here I'm really quite impressed

Some see a doctor twice a week for checkups and rest.

Earth really is a treat so you must come to visit

There's always a natural disasters so you'll be sure not forget it.

See you soon,

Love, Laz

CELTIC DREAMER

To sleep is a blessed gift
Used by all, appreciated by few.
Sleeping restful breathing easy
Dreams of firelights, unearthly cries in the night
Brings sweat to your brow, a candle to your bed,
As you sit up and dream of what was just said.
Nothing more could ever be found
In the nightmare you now try to drown
When you tell yourself it's all unreal.
Things are not always what they seem
When you're in a dream
When you look up and frown, as the sky hits the ground
Memories so define, but this not what you had in mind.
Could you sleep without a dream?
Awaking up in a haze to another sleepy maze
Stumble to your feet. Arms stretched out.
This is what you knew, to always be true.
A dream turned into a nightmare
As you just stop and stare. Who could possibly be there?
Chasing dark shadows
Chasing nightmares

THE GINGERBREAD MAN

I find it easy to provide a story not often recognized

Of the Gingerbread Man.

I find it easy to say how he went away. Known always as

The Gingerbread Man

He was an arbiter and a mystery. When they shot him dead he became history.

His tome says "The Gingerbread Man"

He ate rice cakes and had a very nice face. He never talked but they called him

The Gingerbread Man

He wasn't a bother but they considered him a threat. Because he was rough-like and fished with nets.

He had no name … other than The Gingerbread Man

They were zealots, and he was not. He was compassionate, and for this he was shot?

Why did they call him The Gingerbread Man?

He was not a cookie. He did not bake. He was not made of dough or little round cakes.

But he was The Gingerbread Man.

He crumbled to the ground when they got him from behind.

He was a fast runner but then again so was I.

Maybe that's why they called him The Gingerbread Man.

He was little and smart, just barely 15. They were older and cold of heart.

They didn't give him a chance to scream. I shouted,

'Look out Gingerbread Man".

Boom! They got him. Now he's dead. But I still remember what that town did.

To the Gingerbread Man

They did not bury him. They gave him to the sea. The waves ate him up, Burping a sigh of relief.

This is the demise of The Gingerbread Man.

A DAY AT THE RACES

Faster than lightening or OldGranddad.

Hiccupy Jones, "Here's the pass!"

Front and center not back of the line.

Hiccupy Jones leading in strides.

Legs of steel

The crowd cheers.

The dumb ones betted and are in tears.

Jockey's riding high

Horses fast and low

MumsTheWord just doesn't want to go.

"Ride" They say "Like the wind"

GodSaveTheQueen,

Neck to neck they ride

But no one can keep up with the Jones

So he just flies

To the finish line and beyond.

Tomorrow they'll all be singing a song

About a horse who flew without wings

Who beat every last mare including

GodSaveTheQueen.

FRIENDS????

It's a joy being you

It's a pleasure

But it never last forever

Your friends aren't as true as you thought them to be

They'll leave you in a heartbeat, when they find someone new.

They pretend to like you

When they really don't

Or truly like you but don't want to be around you.

Oh how they adore you…. When no one better is around.

You're quickly forgotten as soon as you're met.

It's a comforting thought … And you'll always have friends…

But you'll always be on the outside looking in.

WHERE IS THE ME OF YESTERYEAR

All alone I live my life

My bleak existence, the hatred, the strife

The tension and pain

This is not what I envisioned for my life.

I think back to yesteryear

Where all was new and clear

Then I didn't even shed a tear

I was strong, unstoppable

Nothing to fear

Where is the me of yesteryear?

When days are longer, when the winds appear

But where is the snow of yesteryear.

A POEM TO POETRY

The poem was mine and mine alone
So I had written so many years ago
There for all to read.
What I knew I could achieve!
Then I became old.
So many things went untold.

TAKERS

Self-righteous and in your face
Noses high, to keep you in your place
I shouted at them "I hate you so much"
My skin was already cold to touch.
No questions asked
No answers gained
What I knew, I knew in vain
My silence for them had to be maintained
To that ended my soul was maimed

CONFESSIONS OF A SHOE HOARDER

I have a problem I must confess
Shoe hoarding is what I like the best
Red heels or green
Flats or floral
My problems are merely moral
The need to buy and fill my closet
The want, to wear and feel amazing
The obsession to spend all my savings
Paving the way to an a new addiction
If only, this was a work of fiction.

WHAT YOU DO TO ME

Shut my mouth
And close my eyes
My hands and feet together tie
My will and freedom
Deprived.
You hate me for what I have
A close relationship with my dad.
What did I do to make you hate me so?
Stranger in my house
A broken family is all I have.
Their divorce
The pain
You're wedding
The sorrow
You fill her shoes and take her place.
You make him laugh and smile
But to me you hate and beguile
I feel trapped
Who do I tell?
When I grow up I won't be you
I won't treat others the way you do
I won't lie and steal their families away
I'll be better because of living with you
I'll be the person I was meant to

Printed in the United States
By Bookmasters